The Little Boy Who Thought

A little boy named Jordan always dreamed of being a superstar. He played basketball every day for hours. He would come home from school and go right back outside to play with his friends until the street lights turned on.

1

Jordan played and watched basketball every chance he could. He wore shorts under his jeans, so he was ready to play at any given moment. He showed a love for the game at an early age.

Little did he know, basketball would impact his life in a variety of positive ways. He traveled all over the country, playing basketball, and building lifelong friendships along the way. In his mind, the path to becoming a superstar had just begun, not realizing there would be many obstacles.

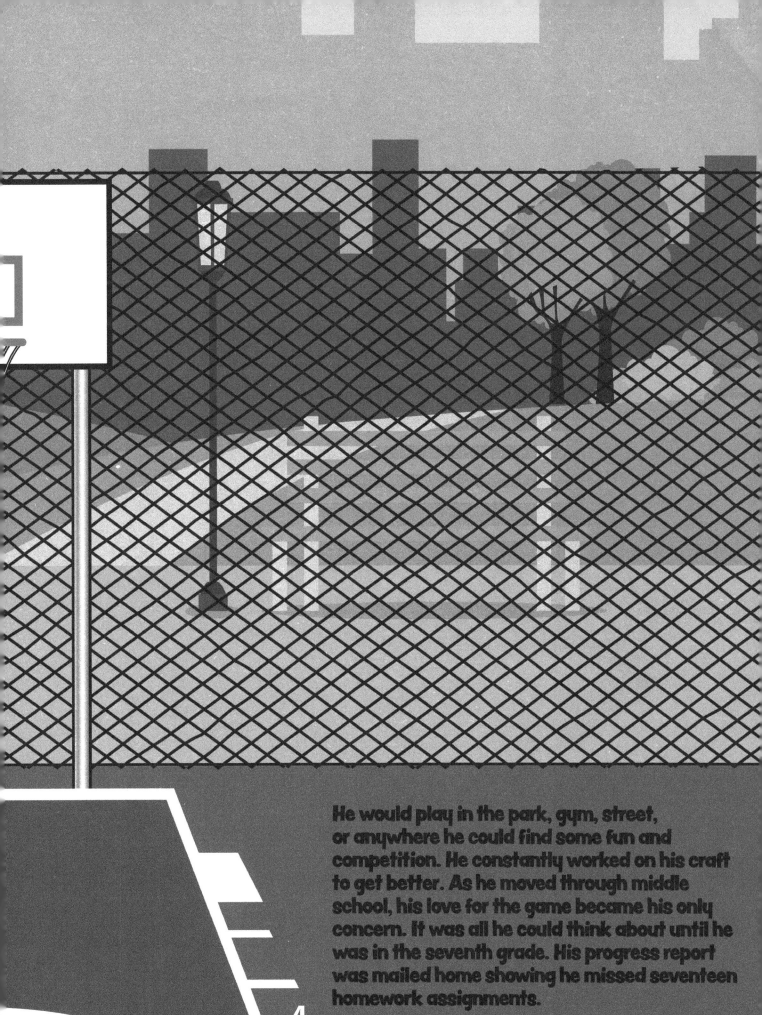

He would play in the park, gym, street, or anywhere he could find some fun and competition. He constantly worked on his craft to get better. As he moved through middle school, his love for the game became his only concern. It was all he could think about until he was in the seventh grade. His progress report was mailed home showing he missed seventeen homework assignments.

When his mother found out, she told him there would be no more basketball until his assignments were up to date. She required him to put the same effort and energy into his schoolwork as he did basketball.

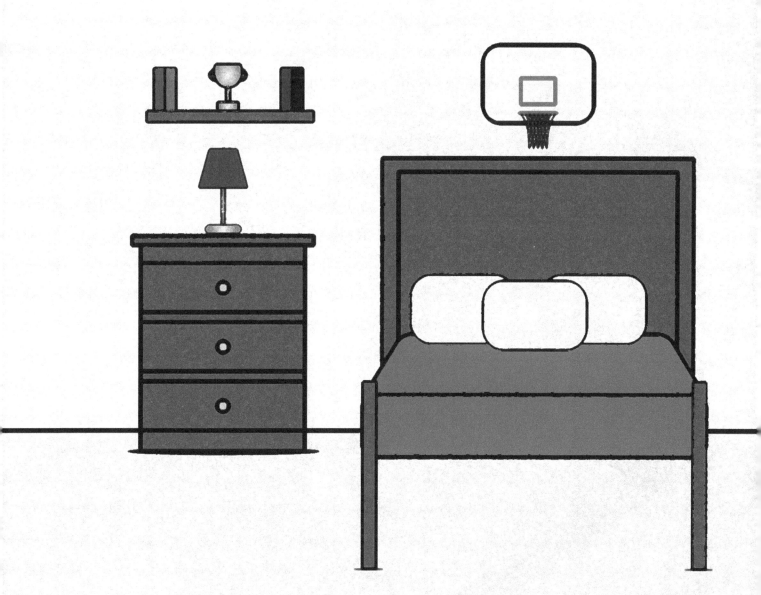

He scrambled and worked with his
teachers to complete his assignments
and vowed never to fall behind again.
He pleaded with his parents to allow
him to play basketball again.

The passion and respect grew even deeper after the
sport he loved was taken away from him for a short time.
He refocused his energy on his classroom performance first,
so that he could continue to excel on the basketball court.

Until this point, education and basketball was all he knew. When Jordan entered high school, balancing education, basketball, and managing friendships were the challenges presented. He started understanding the importance of each aspect and how to prioritize them in his life.

He set goals of making the honor roll, winning state championships, and being a good friend. These goals came with some obstacles.
Teenage obstacles usually revolved around being accepted amongst peers. Missing various teenage activities because of school or sports were some choices he made with a bigger picture in mind.

When Jordan made these tough decisions, he always recalled the harsh lesson he learned in middle school. Losing basketball again was not an option.

As years passed, he started to see the goals he made as a freshman start to form. His senior year, he received honor roll several times, won a high school basketball championship, and earned a college scholarship to play basketball. The choices he made his freshman year, propelled him to the accolades he received his senior year.

He was off to college where he would be faced with new challenges. In college, he was forced to grow up and make decisions based on values instilled by his parents. He slowly became a man managing school and sports. Just when he thought he got the hang of it; his college years were over and graduation was finally here.

Reality hit for the young man when he realized he needed another plan besides professional basketball. The young man was left with a degree that he had no use for and searching for a place in society. He reverted to finding the balance he once needed to get through a difficult time, only this time he was a college graduate and not a little boy.

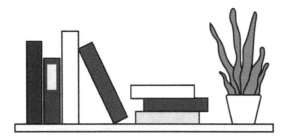

One thing the young man learned from playing basketball and going to college was that relationships were more powerful than anything. He had the will to work and made the best of any situation.

He returned home searching for that one thing that would make his life meaningful. Thinking to himself, *what do I really enjoy? What do I want my career to be?* The young man felt anxious and lost. He started working summer camps, substitute teaching, and volunteering at the local recreation center. These jobs led him to believe that working and leaving an impact should be centered around the youth of his community.

He remembered watching his father build relationships with his students through recreation programs during the summers.

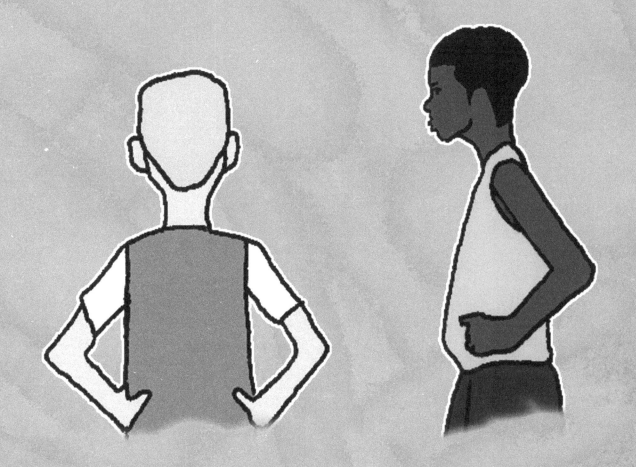

He remembered the excitement he felt watching the older kids when he was younger. He began to think back on all the major men that influenced his life growing up. He decided that he wanted to be a man, a real life figure, that young men could relate to.

He built up the determination to return to school and continued to push through the long nights, while working two jobs. Two and a half years later, he earned a Master's Degree in Early Child Education. This degree felt more purposeful and useful now.

He received his first teaching job working as a
middle school Math teacher. He quickly adapted to his
environment and understood what these students needed.
The students and himself shared similar interests, including
sneakers, music, and sports. These interests were used as
the foundation he needed to properly educate the students
to the best of his ability.

He worked hard for them and genuinely wanted them to succeed. He wanted to continue being a positive role model, so he went searching for more as he pursued another degree in Educational Leadership.

He found a sense of belonging in their teenage minds, while becoming a better man in society. He made sure his impact went beyond the classroom. Becoming a visible presence in the community made the kids further believe in their dreams and relate to him even more.

Today, He continues to work diligently with the youth in his area showing them other possibilities, while still allowing them to chase their dreams. The ability to multitask is a powerful tool that translates across many professions and travels with time.